KU-741-819

# THE HERO

# OTHER SPACE DOG TITLES

# SPACE DOG

# THE HERO

**NATALIE STANDIFORD**
**Illustrated by TONY ROSS**

RED FOX

**A Red Fox Book**

Published by Random House Children's Books
20 Vauxhall Bridge Road, London SW1V 2SA

A division of The Random House Group Ltd
London Melbourne Sydney Auckland
Johannesburg and agencies throughout the world

1 3 5 7 9 10 8 6 4 2
First published by Avon Books Ltd, New York 1991
First published in Great Britain by Hutchinson Children's Books 1992

Red Fox edition 2001

Printed and bound in Denmark by
Nørhaven A/S, Viborg

Papers used by The Random House Group are natural, recyclable products made from wood grown in sustainable forests. The manufacturing processes conform to the environmental regulations of the country of origin.

THE RANDOM HOUSE GROUP Limited Reg. No. 954009

www.randomhouse.co.uk

ISBN 0 09 940476 1

# Contents

# SPACE DOG

## THE HERO

# Chapter 1

# Space Dog Sees Trouble Coming

It was early in the autumn. One night before dinner, Roy Barnes sat in his room doing his homework, but he was having trouble concentrating. It was only the second week of school, and his teacher was already giving them a spelling test.

Roy's dog, Space Dog, was asleep on the bottom part of Roy's bunk bed.

*Rrring!* Suddenly, the alarm clock went off. The noise of the alarm filled the room, but Space Dog didn't move.

At last Roy got up and switched off the alarm. Then he shook Space Dog.

'Hey!' said Roy. 'Wake up!'

Space Dog opened his eyes. 'Huh?' he said.

'You're such a sound sleeper!' said Roy. 'Didn't you hear the alarm?'

'No,' said Space Dog. 'But if it went off, that means it's dinner time. I set the alarm so my stomach would have a little time to wake up and get really hungry.'

'It's *almost* dinner time,' said Roy. He went back to his desk.

'What are you doing?' asked Space Dog.

'Trying to learn,' said Roy. 'I have a spelling test tomorrow, and I don't know these words.'

'I'll test you,' said Space Dog. 'That'll help.' He took Roy's spelling book from the desk and sat on the bed. He looked at the word list and read, 'Bicycle'.

Roy closed his eyes. Then he said, 'B-I-C-Y-C-L-E.'

'Right,' said Space Dog. 'What are you worried about? That's the hardest word on the list.'

Space Dog was able to talk to Roy because he wasn't really a dog. He grew up on the planet Queekrg, far out in space. He was sent on a mission from Queekrg to study the planet Earth. He crash-landed in Roy's back garden, and he and Roy became fast friends.

Space Dog happened to look like a dog,

but he could talk and walk and read like a human. He wanted to keep his mission to Earth a secret, so he always behaved like a dog when anyone except Roy was around. Roy was the only person who knew Space Dog's true identity.

While Roy was spelling 'automobile,' someone knocked on the door of his room. Space Dog slid off the bed quickly and sat in a doggy-like way on the floor.

'Come in,' said Roy, once Space Dog was settled.

Roy's father opened the door. 'Supper's ready,' he said.

'I'm coming,' said Roy.

Mr Barnes went downstairs. As Roy got up from his desk, Space Dog said, 'Can you bring me dinner as soon as possible?'

'It's a deal,' said Roy, and he went downstairs to dinner.

'Don't you have something you want to tell Roy, dear?' said Mrs Barnes. She passed the pork chops to her husband.

'Yes, I do,' said Mr Barnes. 'Roy, I have to go away on business.'

'Where?' said Roy.

'To Manchester,' said Mr Barnes. 'But it's only for a few days. There's nothing to worry about.'

'I'm not worried,' said Roy.

'Roy, you don't have to be brave with us,' said Mrs Barnes. 'It's natural to be a little scared after your home has been broken into. Especially if you know your father isn't going to be around.'

Then Roy knew what his parents were talking about. A few weeks before, while the Barneses were visiting Roy's granny, their house had been broken into. At least that's what Mr and Mrs Barnes thought had happened. The real story was that

Space Dog was the one who had turned the house upside down. He had been left there alone for a few days and made a real mess of things.

'Oh, Dad,' said Roy. 'I don't think there will be another burglar.'

'I hope you're right, Roy,' said Mr Barnes. 'But somebody else's house was broken into last week. It was in the paper.'

'Gosh!' said Roy. 'Was it real burglars?'

'Of course they were real,' said Mr Barnes. 'That's why I'm nervous about you and your mother being alone while I'm away. And that's why I've come up with an idea.'

'What kind of idea?' asked Roy.

'A very practical idea,' said Mr Barnes. 'We've got a dog in the house, haven't we?'

Suddenly Roy *was* worried. 'Yes,' he said slowly.

'Well,' said Mr Barnes, 'Why not put him

to work? He can be our watchdog. He'll guard the house while you and your mother are asleep.'

Roy dropped his fork. 'Space Dog won't like that,' he said. 'I mean, he's probably not very good at watchdogging.'

Mr Barnes's face began to turn red. 'Listen, Roy,' he said sternly. 'That animal costs me a fortune in dog food. It's time he made himself useful around here.'

Roy wanted to tell his father the truth about Space Dog, but he had to hold his tongue. He was the only one who knew that Space Dog never ate a bite of the dog food that the Barneses bought. He ate people food. Roy secretly threw the dog food away.

'But Space Dog doesn't know how to be a watchdog,' said Roy, still hoping to change his father's mind.

'We'll have to teach him,' said Mr Barnes. 'Go to the library and see what you can find.'

'I'm sure Space Dog will do beautifully,' said Mrs Barnes. 'Protecting people comes naturally to dogs.'

Roy swallowed hard. A lot of things came naturally to Space Dog, but protecting Earth people wasn't one of them.

In his room after supper, Roy broke the news to Space Dog. Space Dog did not like Mr Barnes's idea. 'I have to do what?' he asked, hoping he had not heard correctly.

'Guard the house at night,' Roy repeated.

'This is terrible,' said Space Dog. 'I don't know the first thing about guarding a house. And besides, I'm as scared of burglars as your father is.'

'Will you just try it for a little while?' Roy pleaded. 'Who knows? Maybe you'll turn out to be a lean, mean, watchdog machine.'

'Yes,' said Space Dog. 'And you're from the planet Queekrg.'

# Chapter 2

# A Burglar's Worst Enemy

The next day was Friday. Roy went to school and passed his spelling test with flying colours. He also borrowed a book from the library. It was called *How to Turn Your Dog into a Burglar's Worst Enemy*.

He walked home from school with his friend Alice. Alice lived next door. She had a poodle called Blanche. Alice loved her dog. Roy thought the poodle was OK, but Space Dog couldn't stand the sight of her. That was because Blanche had a crush on Space Dog.

'Guess what I have to do tomorrow,' said Roy.

'What?' asked Alice.

'I have to train Space Dog,' said Roy.

'He's already trained,' said Alice.

'I don't mean *that* kind of training,' said Roy. 'I have to train him to be a watchdog.'

'Do you?' said Alice. 'Why?'

'Dad is going away on a business trip,' said Roy. 'He's worried about burglars.'

23

'My parents worry about burglars, too,' said Alice. 'But I know Blanche will protect us.'

'Blanche wouldn't be a good watchdog,' said Roy. 'She's too friendly.'

'She's friendly to *nice* people,' said Alice. 'But she has good instincts. She knows when someone isn't nice. I think all dogs are like that. Isn't Space Dog?'

'Space Dog knows if people aren't nice,' said Roy. 'But he never growls or barks. I don't think a burglar would ever be afraid of him.'

'He must be a little bit of a watchdog,' said Alice. 'Doesn't he ever chase squirrels or growl at other dogs?'

'Never,' said Roy.

'Well,' said Alice, 'I just hope no one ever breaks into your house.'

'Me too,' said Roy.

Mr Barnes left for Manchester the next morning. 'Take good care of the family,' he said to Space Dog.

Space Dog shivered and hoped no one noticed. Mr Barnes gave Roy and Mrs Barnes a kiss and drove off to the station.

Roy spent the afternoon in Space Dog's kennel. He wanted Space Dog to study the new library book.

'I don't even like the title of this book,'

26

said Space Dog. '*How to Turn Your Dog into a Burglar's Worst Enemy.* I'm *afraid* of burglars!'

'I know,' said Roy. 'Burglars are frightening. But you have to think about this watchdog business in a new way. Think of all the great stories about dog heroes. Think of Lassie. Think of all the dogs who protect people. You could be like them – a dog hero who lays his life on the line for the people he loves.'

As Roy spoke, Space Dog sat a little taller and straighter beside him. 'Yes, I can see it now,' said Space Dog. 'I could be part of the long tradition of gallant Earth heroes. Like King Arthur, or Superman, or the first astronauts . . .'

Suddenly Space Dog shook his head and came to his senses. 'Are you crazy?' he said to Roy. 'Now you've got me talking nonsense. I don't *want* to be a hero. I'm just a humble scientist from Queekrg, spending some time on Earth. I wasn't cut out to be a crime-stopper.'

'It won't be too bad,' said Roy. 'If you learn a few of the tricks in this book, maybe you'll feel better.'

'I learned one good trick on Queekrg,' said Space Dog. He began to tell a story. 'One year when I was at school, somebody started stealing my lunch. My mother always packed a really good lunch for me. And the best things in my lunch box were the pefts.'

'What's a peft?' asked Roy.

'It's a yummy dessert. It's like a cake, only rubbery. It's round like a ball, with a powdery filling inside.'

'It sounds weird,' said Roy.

'It was the greatest,' said Space Dog. 'Anyway, at school we kept our lunches in mini-refrigerators.'

'Wow!' said Roy. 'You had your own refrigerators?'

'Yes,' said Space Dog. 'Each pupil had one under his seat. And this kid who sat next to me, Terg, always managed to get into my fridge and steal my pefts. It was terrible. It was especially terrible because my mother made the best pefts on the planet!'

'So what did you do?' asked Roy.

'I set a trap for the sneaky little devil,' said Space Dog. 'Before school one day, I sliced open my peft and emptied out all the sugary powder—into my mouth, of course. Then I filled it with the worst powdery stuff I could think of.'

'What was that?' asked Roy.

'Blorp,' said Space Dog. 'It's a kind of spice. It is like garlic, only stronger.'

'Yuk!' said Roy.

'Yuk is right,' said Space Dog. 'I put the

peft filled with blorp in my lunch box and took it to school. Then I put the whole thing in my fridge.'

Space Dog smiled. Then he went on. 'I didn't see Terg steal the peft, but by lunchtime, when I opened my box, it was gone. I sat near Terg in the dining room and kept my eye on him. After a while I saw him take a peft out of his lunch box.'

'Then what happened?' asked Roy.

'Some of the other kids noticed that Terg had a peft. He waved it around to make them jealous. Then he opened his mouth wide and took a big bite.'

'And?'

'And spat it out— right on to the table! It was disgusting. He got into big trouble with the teacher.'

'Did he say anything to you?' asked Roy.

'He didn't dare,' said Space Dog. 'He just

gave me a dirty look and drank a lot of garzle juice. But he never stole a peft again!'

'That was a good story,' said Roy. 'But I don't think pefts and garzle juice have anything to do with you being a watchdog.'

'I suppose not,' said Space Dog. 'Too bad. What does it say in that book of yours, anyway?'

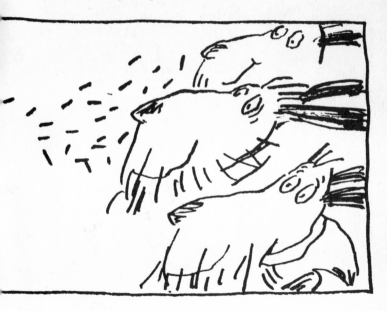

## Chapter 3

# A Lesson from Blanche

Roy and Space Dog were still in the kennel. Roy sat on the floor. Space Dog lay on his side, his head propped up with his hand. He did not look much like a dog.

'Let's see,' said Roy. 'Step one. The book says a good watchdog must be able to sniff out troublemakers.'

'Step one is out,' said Space Dog. 'You know me. The only thing I'm good at sniffing out is food.' He thought for a minute. 'Let's say, in our case, the burglar has already done something to show he's a troublemaker. I don't have to sniff him out because I know he's a burglar. He's already tried to get into the house. So, what happens next?'

Roy looked at the book. 'Step two is growl at the burglar and try to scare him away. Well, that's a tough one. We already know you can't growl.'

'Sad, but true,' said Space Dog.

'Step three is you're supposed to bark,' said Roy. 'To wake up the people in the house.'

Space Dog read aloud over Roy's shoulder. '"The bark acts as an alarm,"' Space Dog read. '"It alerts the dog's owners so that they know there is trouble afoot." Good luck to me.'

'I've never heard you bark,' said Roy. 'Do you think you can?'

'Probably not,' said Space Dog. 'On Queekrg, if someone made a barking sound, everyone would think he was crazy.'

'Most people here don't bark either,' said Roy. 'But no one thinks twice if a dog barks. And everyone on Earth thinks *you're a dog.*'

'You don't have to remind me,' said Space Dog.

'Well, go ahead,' said Roy. 'Let's hear you bark.'

'Oh, Roy,' said Space Dog. 'This really puts me on the spot. I'm embarrassed.'

'There's nothing to be embarrassed about,' said Roy. 'I don't mind barking. Watch.' Roy paused a moment. '*Ruff! Ruff!*' he barked. Then he said calmly, 'See? Nothing to it!'

'That was good, Roy,' said Space Dog. 'Now flap your arms like a chicken.'

'I don't want to,' said Roy.

'Please?' said Space Dog. 'If you flap your arms like a chicken, I promise to bark.'

'I can't believe this,' said Roy. 'OK. Here goes.' Roy knelt and bent his arms at the elbow. Then he flapped them like a chicken and said, *'Buck-buck-buck!'*

Space Dog started to laugh, and Roy laughed with him. Suddenly Space Dog stopped laughing. He quickly rolled onto his stomach and pulled up his hind legs. He was trying to look like a dog.

Roy turned around and saw Alice and Blanche peering in the door of the kennel.

'Gosh, Roy,' said Alice. 'What are you doing?'

'Don't you ever knock?' said Roy.

'I didn't know I had to knock,' said Alice. 'It's just a kennel. But, wow, you've got a lot of stuff in here.' She looked at the stacks of books and papers. Luckily, Space Dog had put his portable computer away.

'This is not just a kennel,' said Roy. 'It is also my secret den. And you and Blanche are not allowed inside!'

'OK, OK,' said Alice, as Roy pushed her out of the door. 'You don't have to shove.'

Roy and Space Dog followed Alice out of the kennel. Roy closed the door behind them. The minute they were all outside, Blanche walked up to Space Dog, wagging her tail happily.

Space Dog pulled away from her. *Please, Roy!* he begged silently. *Get Blanche out of here!*

It was Alice who came to Space Dog's

rescue. 'No, Blanche,' she said, pulling her dog away. 'Space Dog doesn't like to rub noses.'

'Thanks, Alice,' said Roy. 'I'm sorry I got cross about the kennel. It's just that some things are really secret, you know?'

'I know,' said Alice. 'But can I ask you one question?'

'What?'

'Why were you behaving like a chicken in there?'

'I was—uh—' Roy stammered. 'I was doing some exercises.'

'Oh,' said Alice. 'Well, how's the watch-dog training going?'

'Not so well,' said Roy.

'I started thinking after we talked yesterday,' said Alice. 'Blanche needs to learn more about being a watchdog, too. So I taught her some new tricks. Want to see them?'

'OK,' said Roy.

'Well, here goes,' said Alice.

Alice held up a sort of rag doll made of old socks. The sock doll had a face drawn on it with magic marker.

'I made this,' said Alice. 'It's supposed to be a burglar. Now watch.'

Alice shook the doll in Blanche's face and said in a low, mean voice, 'Heh, heh, heh! I'm a horrible burglar, and I'm coming to rob your house!'

Blanche began to growl.

Alice threw the sock doll on the ground. 'Get the burglar, Blanche!' she said. 'Get him, girl!'

Growling, Blanche pounced on the socks. She grabbed them with her teeth and began to tear them up. 'Isn't she great?' said Alice. 'The only bad thing is that I have to keep making new dolls. Blanche rips them to shreds.'

'Wow!' said Roy. 'She really has the killer instinct. Or else she just likes tearing up socks.'

Space Dog was watching Blanche. He rolled his eyes. *That poodle is a dumbo*, he said to himself. *She fights socks as though they were going to fight her back.*

Alice went to Blanche and tried to get the burglar doll away from her. 'Give it to me, Blanchie,' she said. But Blanche held on. Alice tugged, but the dog would not let go. Finally Alice had to force Blanche's mouth open. The sock doll fell to the ground. By then, it was nothing but rags. Alice picked it up and handed it to Roy.

'Want to try the burglar with Space Dog?' she asked.

Roy hesitated. 'Well . . .' he said.

'Come on,' said Alice. 'Try it. Maybe Space Dog will surprise you.'

47

'OK,' said Roy. He shook what was left of the burglar doll in front of Space Dog. Little droplets flew out of it. 'It's kind of wet,' said Roy.

Space Dog's stomach turned. He knew why the rags were wet. They had been in Blanche's mouth.

Roy held the tattered doll closer and closer to Space Dog. 'Here comes a burglar, Space Dog,' he said. 'He's coming to get you!'

Space Dog started to back away from Roy. The closer Roy came, the more Space Dog backed away. Finally Roy tossed the burglar on the ground and said, 'Go get him, Space Dog!'

Space Dog looked up at Roy. Then he sat down quietly.

'Wow,' said Alice. 'He really is a hopeless case, isn't he?'

'Yes,' said Roy. 'But I like him anyway.'

## Chapter 4

# Space Dog's First Night on the Job

Roy and Space Dog sat in Roy's room after supper.

'Well,' said Roy, 'tonight's your first night on duty.' He tried to sound cheerful.

Space Dog looked miserable. 'What if something goes wrong?' he said. 'I'm a heavy sleeper. A burglar could clean the house out, and I would probably sleep though it.'

'No you wouldn't,' said Roy. 'But we won't take any chances. Let's work out just what you have to do. First of all, you have to stay downstairs all night.'

'What?' said Space Dog. 'By myself?'

'Well . . .'

'ALONE?' said Space Dog with horror in his voice.

Roy thought quickly. Space Dog was getting upset. If he got too upset, he might leave. He might repair his little spaceship and disappear. Roy couldn't let that happen.

'I'll stay downstairs with you,' said Roy. 'At least for tonight.'

'Good,' said Space Dog. He sounded relieved. 'What do we do if a burglar comes?'

'You bark, I suppose,' Roy answered.

'I'd better practise,' said Space Dog. 'How does it go again?'

'*Ruff! Ruff!*' barked Roy.

'*Bark, bark*,' said Space Dog. 'How was that?'

'No good,' said Roy. 'Worse than your growl.'

'What am I going to do?' said Space Dog. 'I admit it, Roy. I'm scared.'

'If we're together, you won't be scared,' said Roy.

Space Dog smiled at him, 'You're right,' he said. 'You're a real friend, Roy. Thanks'.

'No problem,' said Roy. 'I always wanted to spend the night downstairs. But we'll have to be very quiet. Mum will kill me if she catches me out of bed.'

'OK,' said Space Dog. 'We'll be quiet.' Suddenly he thought of a new problem. 'Roy, do watchdogs stay awake all night?'

Roy sighed. 'I think they're supposed to,' he said.

'I can't do that,' said Space Dog. 'I'm sure I'll fall asleep.'

'Don't worry,' Roy said quickly. 'I'll help you stay awake. It won't be too hard.'

Roy patted his friend and sighed. It was important to keep Space Dog happy, but he didn't feel he was doing a very good job.

That night, Space Dog stayed downstairs when Roy went up to bed. In her son's bedroom, Mrs Barnes kissed Roy good night and turned off the light. Then she went back downstairs. Roy lay in the dark, trying to stay awake. He waited for ever for his mother to come up the stairs again.

At last Mrs Barnes turned out the lights

in the living room and came up. 'Good night, Space Dog,' she said. 'Guard us well!'

Space Dog moaned. *I hope Roy hurries*, he said to himself.

A few minutes later, Roy got out of bed and tiptoed down the stairs. The whole house was dark. When he got downstairs, he whispered, '*Psst!* Space Dog!'

'Over here!' Space Dog whispered back. He was in the living room.

Roy joined him on the sofa. 'How's it going?' he asked.

'OK,' said Space Dog. 'But I'm sleepy already. And it's only eleven o'clock!'

The two friends sat in the dark, saying nothing. The clock on the mantelpiece went *tick tick tick*. The refrigerator hummed in the kitchen. Everything else was quiet.

'What should we do?' Roy whispered.

'I don't know,' said Space Dog. 'But we have to find something to keep us awake.'

'Should we play a game?' asked Roy.

'Too dark,' said Space Dog.

'Should we watch TV?' asked Roy.

'Too noisy,' said Space Dog.

They sat on the sofa, twiddling their thumbs. Space Dog yawned.

'Maybe we can turn on a teeny, weeny little light somewhere,' said Roy. 'Then we could work out something to do.'

'Good idea,' said Space Dog. 'Let's find a teeny light.'

They settled on a reading lamp in the study. Space Dog waited while Roy found some sheets of paper. Then Roy showed Space Dog how to make paper aeroplanes. Each time they finished a plane, they flew it quietly over the rug.

In the middle of making planes, Space Dog suddenly froze.

'What's wrong?' asked Roy.

'Did you hear that?' said Space Dog.

'What?'

'That noise,' said Space Dog.

'What noise?'

Just then there was a little crash. It sounded like metal.

'*That* noise,' said Space Dog.

'Yikes!' said Roy. 'What is it?'

'I don't know,' said Space Dog. 'It came from the back of the house.'

They heard the sound again, this time a little louder. Space Dog and Roy grabbed each other.

'Is this it?' said Space Dog. 'Is the burglar here?'

'I don't know,' said Roy. 'You'd better go and look.'

'*Me?*' said Space Dog. 'Why me?'

'You're the watchdog,' said Roy, hoping he could stay just where he was.

*Crash. Bump.* Then there was the sound of paper rustling.

'Help!' whispered Space Dog. 'What should we do?'

'Let's both go and see what it is,' said Roy.

'OK,' said Space Dog.

Still holding on to each other, Space Dog and Roy tiptoed into the dark kitchen. They heard more noises—coming from outside the back door. Something or someone was definitely out there!

## Chapter 5

# Who's There?

Space Dog and Roy tiptoed over to the kitchen window and slowly peered out. The dustbin had tipped over, and the lid had fallen off. Something furry had its head inside it.

'What's that?' whispered Space Dog.

'It's not a burglar!' said Roy happily. 'It's just a fox. That's an animal that gets into people's rubbish.'

Space Dog breathed a sigh of relief. 'Is that all?' he said. 'Thank goodness. Let's go back to the den.'

'Wait,' said Roy. 'Maybe foxes are supposed to be part of your job. They leave rubbish all over the garden. Maybe my mum thinks you'll go out of your dog door and chase them away.'

'*You* chase that fox away,' said Space Dog. 'He's pretty big.'

'Well, we've got to do something,' said Roy.

'What about the paper aeroplanes?' said Space Dog. 'They're nice and pointy. We could aim them at the fox.'

'And they don't make any noise,' said Roy. 'Good idea.' He and Space Dog went back to the study. They took a pile of aeroplanes and brought them into the kitchen. Then they quietly opened the back door.

The fox didn't even look up. He was busy with the rubbish. Space Dog and Roy stood in the doorway and aimed. Roy flew the first plane. It missed. Then Space Dog tried. His plane bopped the fox's side. 'Got him!' said Space Dog. The fox looked up. His eyes glowed yellow.

Roy threw another plane. It landed at the fox's feet. The animal backed away a little.

After a few more aeroplanes, the fox finally got the message. He sped away, off to dig in someone else's rubbish. Roy and Space Dog shook hand and paw.

'Let's play Old Maid,' said Space Dog. 'I'll get the cards.'

'Not yet,' said Roy. 'We have to tidy up first.'

'You mean go out there and pick up that filthy rubbish?' said Space Dog.

'Yes,' Roy insisted. 'My mother is going to think something's very wrong if the garden is covered with rubbish and paper aeroplanes.'

Quiet as mice they crept outside and gingerly picked up the rubbish. When they

had finished, they went inside and locked the door behind them.

'I've got to wash,' said Space Dog.

'OK,' said Roy. 'But do it really, really, quietly.'

They washed their hands in a trickle of water at the kitchen sink. Then they found the cards and tiptoed back to the study. Many hours and card games later, the sky began to grow light.

'I'd better go upstairs now,' said Roy. 'It's almost morning. Mum will be getting up. Will you be OK by yourself now?'

'Yes,' said Space Dog. 'As long as it's light outside I'm not scared. Burglars don't usually come in the morning, do they?'

'I don't think so,' said Roy. 'Well, see you later.'

'See you,' said Space Dog.

Roy tiptoed upstairs to his room. He got into bed and fell asleep before his head hit the pillow.

An hour later, Mrs Barnes woke up. When she went downstairs to start the coffee, she found her watchdog sound asleep.

## Chapter 6

# Sleepy Sunday

That morning Roy slept and slept. Even though it was Sunday and Roy didn't have to get up, his mother began to think that he was ill. Finally she went to his room to wake him.

'Roy?' said Mrs Barnes. 'Roy?'

Roy only turned in his sleep.

'Roy?' Mrs Barnes shook her son lightly.

Roy opened his eyes. 'What? Is there a burglar?' he said.

'No, Roy,' said Mrs Barnes. 'No burglar. I was just wondering if you were all right.'

'Oh,' said Roy. He rubbed his eyes and sat up in bed. 'I'm all right,' he said. 'Just tired.'

'That's not like you,' said Mrs Barnes. 'Are you sure you're not sickening for something?'

'No, no!' said Roy, thinking quickly. 'It's probably just, you know, getting used to school again and everything.'

Mrs Barnes felt Roy's forehead. 'You feel all right,' she said. 'But tonight you're going to bed early, young man. You've got

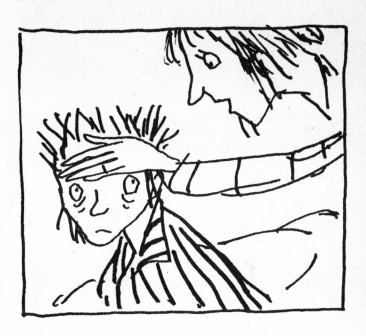

school tomorrow, you know.'

'I know, Mum,' said Roy. 'I promise to get a good night's sleep tonight.'

'Good boy,' said Mrs Barnes. 'Now, come downstairs and have some lunch—or breakfast, if you want.'

'OK,' said Roy.

When Roy went downstairs, he found Space Dog asleep on the living-room floor. *I'd like to curl up next to him*, Roy thought with a yawn.

The smell of spaghetti and meatballs woke Space Dog just before supper. He walked into the kitchen just as Roy and his mother were sitting down to eat. Roy's face lit up when he saw Space Dog.

'Hi, old pal,' said Roy.

Space Dog gave Roy a wink as he walked through the kitchen. Then he went out through the swinging dog door to the back garden.

After supper Roy took some leftover spaghetti out to the kennel. He knocked his secret code on the kennel door—two long knocks and two short.

'I smell supper,' Space Dog said. 'Come in.'

Roy crawled into the kennel. 'Hi, Space Dog,' he said, handing over the food. 'I'm glad you're up. I missed you this afternoon.'

'Well, now we have all night together,' said Space Dog. 'I'm ready to beat you in another round of Old Maid.' He speared a meatball with his fork and popped it into his mouth. 'Mmm,' he said. 'My compliments to the chef.'

Roy was sitting cross-legged. He looked down at his trainer. 'There's one little problem,' he said. 'I can't stay with you tonight. I've got school tomorrow.'

Space Dog stopped eating and looked at Roy. 'You mean I have to stay up all night by myself?' He dropped his fork. 'I've just lost my appetite.'

'Don't get upset, Space Dog,' said Roy.

'Don't get upset?' Space Dog echoed. 'What's there not to get upset about? Being downstairs is bad enough, but staying up all night alone is a nightmare!'

'Maybe it's OK if you go to sleep tonight,' said Roy. 'As long as you're downstairs.'

'Thank goodness,' said Space Dog. 'But I still have to stay by myself, right?'

'Right,' said Roy.

Space Dog looked unhappy again. Roy tried to think of a way to make him feel better. 'As soon as my father gets home,' he said, 'I'll tell him you have to sleep in my room again—because I just can't sleep without you!'

# Chapter 7

# Space Dog Stands Alone

Roy and Space Dog were in Roy's room. Roy was getting ready for bed.

'It's not fair,' said Space Dog, watching Roy get into his pyjamas. 'You can sleep in a nice warm bed. I have to go downstairs and listen for burglars. What a world.'

Just then there was a knock on the bedroom door. 'Come in,' said Roy.

It was Mrs Barnes. 'Almost ready for bed, Roy?' she said.

'Yes, Mum,' said Roy.

'Good,' said Mrs Barnes. 'I'll take the dog

downstairs. Come on, Space Dog. Out you go.'

Space Dog gave Roy his saddest look. Then Mrs Barnes shooed him out of the room.

'Good night, Space Dog,' Roy called after him.

*Sleep tight, Roy, you lucky duck*, Space Dog said to himself.

For the next two nights Roy slept upstairs while Space Dog dozed on the floor downstairs. Poor Space Dog would wake up from time to time, hearing one kind of noise or another. He began having bad dreams. During the day he was tired and miserable. Roy was worried about him.

On Wednesday night Space Dog waited downstairs as usual while Mrs Barnes turned on the dishwasher and turned off the lights. It wasn't long before she went upstairs to bed. Soon the house was as quiet as a church.

Space Dog made his rounds. He dragged himself from room to room. He checked the windows and doors to make sure they were locked.

*Now what?* he wondered. *I know. A little game of patience.*

Space Dog sat on the floor and played cards. He played game after game. But he didn't do very well. He was too tired to

concentrate. And it was lonely without Roy.

He was just getting up to make himself a little snack when he heard a noise. He froze. His heart pounded madly. But he told himself to calm down. *It's probably just another fox*, he thought. *Don't panic.*

The house was still. Space Dog listened for more noises. Then he heard something that sounded like footsteps coming up the front path.

Space Dog hugged himself hard. *Oh no!* he thought. *I'm too young to die! Somebody do something!*

Space Dog was standing in the front hall. Suddenly he saw the doorknob begin to turn. *Help!* thought Space Dog. *It's a burglar trying to get in! I have to stop him!*

The doorknob was rattling. Quickly

Space Dog shoved the hall table in front of the door.

*Quick! What would a watchdog do?* Space Dog wondered frantically.

Then he answered himself. *Who cares what a watchdog would do!* he thought. *I'm calling the police!*

He raced to the telephone and dialled 999. 'Get me the police!' he whispered into the phone. He gave the Barneses' address.

'We already have a car in the area,' said

the operator. 'The officers should arrive any minute.'

'Thank you!' said Space Dog, and hung up the phone. He peeped into the hallway. The intruder had opened the door. He was slowly pushing it open, but the table was still in the way.

The robber started ringing the doorbell. 'Hey!' he shouted. 'Will somebody let me in?'

A chill ran down Space Dog's spine. He knew that voice. That wasn't a robber! That was Mr Barnes!

Then Space Dog heard a siren. *Oh, no!* he thought. *Here come the police!*

He watched out of the window as a police car pulled up in front of the house. Two officers ran up the front path and grabbed Mr Barnes.

Space Dog darted to the front door and pulled the table away from it. The door swung open. Mr Barnes was shouting at the police officers. 'What are you doing? This is my house!'

Roy and Mrs Barnes both came running downstairs. 'Barney!' said Mrs Barnes when she saw her husband and the police. 'What on *earth* is going on?'

'Excuse us, ma'am,' said one of the police officers. 'We caught this man breaking into your house.'

'Breaking in?' said Mrs Barnes. 'But he lives here!'

'Does he?' said the officer.

'That's what I was trying to tell you!' said Mr Barnes, angrily.

The two officers looked confused. 'But someone called us and reported a break-in,' said the second officer.

Roy looked at Space Dog. Space Dog shrugged. He stared at the ceiling.

Mrs Barnes went up to Mr Barnes and kissed him. 'Officers, this is my husband,' she said. 'You can release him.'

The policemen had been holding Mr Barnes by the arms. 'We're very sorry, sir,' said the first officer, letting go of the suspect. 'I think there must have been a mistake, but we did get a call.'

'One of the neighbours must have called you,' said Mr Barnes, 'but you certainly didn't waste any time jumping to conclusions.'

'That's all right,' said Mrs Barnes. 'You were just doing your job.'

Mr Barnes rubbed his arm. 'Yes,' he said. 'But next time, be careful before you start grabbing people!'

'Yes, sir. Sorry, sir,' said the policemen. 'Goodnight.'

The police officers left. Mr Barnes picked up his suitcase and went inside the house. Mrs Barnes and Roy hugged him.

'Welcome home, Dad!' said Roy.

'What a night!' said Mr Barnes. Then he saw Space Dog. 'By the way. What has *he* been doing all this time?' he said. 'I could

have been a burglar for all this dog knew, but he didn't bark once. Some watchdog!'

'That's not right, Dad,' said Roy. 'Space Dog took good care of us while you were gone. Didn't he, Mum?'

'I suppose so, Roy,' said Mrs Barnes. 'It's hard to say.'

'He did,' said Roy. 'I know he did.'

'It doesn't matter any more,' said Mr Barnes. 'From now on, we won't need a watchdog.'

'Won't we?' said Roy happily. Space Dog's ears perked up.

'No,' said Mr Barnes. 'I've decided to put in a burglar alarm.'

'Have you?' said Mrs Barnes.

'Yes,' said Mr Barnes.

'Can Space Dog sleep in my room again?' said Roy.

'I don't see why not,' said Mrs Barnes.

'Hurray!' said Roy.

'Speaking of sleep,' said Mrs Barnes, 'it's awfully late. You'd better get to bed, Roy.'

Roy kissed his parents good night. Then he and Space Dog went upstairs.

Once they were alone together, settling into bed, Roy said to Space Dog, 'You called the police, didn't you?'

'Yes,' said Space Dog. 'I didn't know your father was coming home tonight. I thought he was a burglar. What a lousy watchdog I am!'

'No, you're not,' said Roy. 'You're the greatest! You stayed up all night just to keep us safe. It's not your fault there wasn't a real burglar. If a burglar *had* come, you would have been a hero.'

'Maybe you're right,' said Space Dog. 'If your dad had been a burglar, I would have helped catch him. I would have been a hero.'

'Of course I'm right,' said Roy sleepily.

Space Dog snuggled down under the covers. 'Gosh, I am glad I'm not downstairs,' he said. 'It's good to be back in my own cosy bed.'

## Chapter 8

# The Burglar Alarm

The very next day while Roy was at school, the burglar alarm people came and put in the new system. Mr Barnes stayed away from the office to watch the alarm being installed. When Roy came home, his father showed him how it worked.

'I bought the best system they had,' said Mr Barnes as he played with the buttons and lights. 'But remember, it's not a toy.'

'OK,' said Roy.

Mr Barnes pointed to a little hole in the wall at the bottom of the stairs. 'When the alarm is on,' he said, 'a laser beam will shoot out of here. If anybody tries to walk up the stairs at night, the alarm will go off. Have you got that?'

'Yes, Dad,' said Roy.

'Just then Mrs Barnes came out of the kitchen. 'I've just finished talking to all the neighbours,' she said. 'One or two say they heard the sirens last night, but not one of

them called the police.'

'Whoever called doesn't want to admit it,' said Mr Barnes. 'They don't want to look silly.'

'You may be right, dear,' said Roy's mother.

'Dad,' said Roy, 'Can I go out and play now?'

'You haven't done your homework yet,' said Mr Barnes.

'I'll do it later,' said Roy.

'Oh, no you won't,' said Mr Barnes. 'You'll go upstairs and do it right now.'

'Dad!' said Roy.

'Barney,' said Mrs Barnes. 'Let him go outside. He needs a chance to relax after last night. It's frightening to have the police arrive at midnight—even if it was a false alarm.'

'Oh, all right,' said Mr Barnes. 'I'm sorry, Roy. Go out and play.'

'Thanks, Dad,' said Roy. He ran through the kitchen and out of the back door. He saw Alice and Blanche playing next door.

'Hi, Roy!' called Alice. 'Watch this!' She tossed a doggie treat up in the air. Blanche jumped up high, wiggled three times like a hula dancer and caught the treat. Then she ate it.

'Great, huh?' said Alice.

'Yeah,' said Roy. 'That's a good trick.'

'I bet Space Dog can't do that,' said Alice.

'I bet you're right,' said Roy.

'I bet you wish he *could* do it,' said Alice.

'Not really,' said Roy. 'There are other things I like about Space Dog.'

'Like what?' asked Alice.

'For one thing, he doesn't drool,' said Roy.

That made Alice mad. She threw a doggie treat at Roy. 'You dodo,' she said. 'Dogs are *supposed* to drool.'

'Maybe,' said Roy. 'But it's nicer when they don't. See you.'

'See you, Roy.'

Roy knocked his secret knock on the kennel door. 'Come in,' said Space Dog.

Roy went in on all fours. 'Hi,' he said. 'What are you doing?'

'I'm reading the encyclopedia. The section about crime on Earth. I decided I have first-hand experience of it now.'

Roy shook his head. 'I wish I could tell Alice what an amazing dog you are,' he said. 'She was just showing off with Blanche again.'

'I know,' said Space Dog. 'But that's the way it goes. Just think of me the way you think of Superman.'

'What do you mean?' asked Roy.

'Well,' said Space Dog, '*we* know I'm special, like Superman. But Alice thinks I'm just ordinary, like Clark Kent. Get it?'

'Hmm,' said Roy. 'I never thought of it that way before.'


That night the Barnes family went to bed early. But Space Dog had trouble getting to sleep. Staying up half the night for most of the week had thrown him off course.

He listened to Roy's slow, steady breathing and knew Roy was asleep. He went out in the hall and heard the low rumble of Mr Barnes's snores.

*I know what I need*, thought Space Dog.
*A little snack.*

Space Dog tiptoed down the stairs, trying not to make them creak. But when he got to the foot of the stairs . . .

RRRRRIIIIIIINNNNNNNNNGGGGGG!!!!

All the Barneses ran out onto the upstairs landing. 'Call the police!' shouted

Mr Barnes. Roy looked down and saw Space Dog shaking at the bottom of the stairs. Mrs Barnes saw him, too. She calmly went to a box on the wall upstairs and switched off the alarm. The house was suddenly quiet.

'Calm down, Barney,' said Mrs Barnes. 'Look.' She pointed to Space Dog. 'It's not a burglar. It's our watchdog.'

Space Dog lay down and put his paws

over his eyes. Roy went downstairs to pat him.

'But Space Dog couldn't have got in the way of that laser beam,' said Mr Barnes. 'I made sure it was set high enough so that he could go underneath.'

Roy's heart gave a thump. He knew Space Dog must have set off the alarm by walking like a person, on two feet. Maybe his father would finally guess there was something strange going on.

But Mr Barnes just threw up his hands. 'That dog,' he said sleepily, heading back to bed. 'Nothing but trouble. Maybe we won't use the laser beam after all. The door alarm is enough.'

Roy patted Space Dog. 'Dad thinks you're Clark Kent,' he said. 'But don't worry. I know you're Superman.'

Whatever you like to read, Red Fox has got the story for you. Why not choose another book from our range of Animal Stories, Funny Stories or Fantastic Stories? Reading has never been so much fun!

# Red Fox Animal Stories

**FOWL PEST**
(Shortlisted for the Smarties Prize)
James Andrew Hall
Amy Pickett wants to be a chicken! Seriously! Understandably her family aren't too keen on the idea. Even Amy's best friend, Clarice, thinks she's unhinged. Then Madam Marvel comes to town and strange feathery things begin to happen.
*A Fantastic tale, full of jokes*
CHILD EDUCATION
0 09 940182 7     £2.99

**OMELETTE: A CHICKEN IN PERIL**
Gareth Owen
Suddenly the egg broke! A young chicken popped his head out of the crack to see - with horror - the looming shape of a frying pan. And so Omelette was launched into the world. This is just the beginning of the young chicken's adventures, and with so many enemies on the loose, Omelette really needs his wits about him.
0 09 940013 8     £2.99

**ESCAPE TO THE WILD**
Colin Dann
Eric made up his mind. He would go to the pet shop, open the cages and let the little troupe of animals escape to the wild.
*Readers will find the book unputdownable*
GROWING POINT
0 09 940063 4     £2.99

**SEAL SECRET**
Aidan Chambers
William is really fed up on holiday in Wales until Gwyn, the boy from the nearby farm, shows him the seal lying in a cave. Gwn knows exactly what he is going to do with it; William knows he has to stop him...
0 09 999150 0     £2.99

## RED FOX READ ALONE

Based on the stories by

### HUGH LOFTING

# Doctor Dolittle

### IT TAKES A SPECIAL BOOK TO BE A RED FOX READ ALONE!

Doctor Dolittle is at last brought to life for the youngest reader in these new Doctor Dolittle books based on Hugh Lofting's original stories. Theses titles will amuse and entertain a new generation of Doctor Dolittle fans.

Doctor Dolittle's First Adventure

Doctor Dolittle and the Lighthouse

Doctor Dolittle and the Ambulance

Doctor Dolittle takes Charge

# Flossie Teacake's

## BY HUNTER DAVIES

**It's so unfair!** Flossie Teacake is always watching her older brother and sister do things that she is not allowed to do herself. But all her dreams come true when she tries on her sister Bella's fur coat, and is magically transformed from a timid ten-year-old to an extremely exciting eighteen-year-old with the world at her feet. Watch out everyone, Flossie is determined to have as much fun as possible...

**Read about Flossie's many madcap adventures in these fantastic books**

Flossie Teacake's Fur Coat
0 09 996710 3  £3.99

Flossie Teacake Again
0 09 996720 0  £3.99

Flossie Teacake Strikes Back
0 09 996730 8  £3.99

Flossie Teacake wins the Lottery
0 09 971151 6  £3.99

Flossie Teacake's Holiday
0 09 940372 2  £3.99